# The Littlest Mountain

For Deb for her faith and friendship — B.R.

For Rabbi Yael Romer and the congregation
of Temple Emanuel of Kingston, New York — M.H.



KAR-BEN Publishing
A division of Lerner Publishing Group, Inc.
241 First Avenue North
Minneapolis, MN 55401 U.S.A.
1-800-4KARBEN

Website address: www.karben.com

Library of Congress Cataloging-in-Publication Data

Rosenstock, Barb.
The littlest mountain / by Barb Rosenstock ; illustrated by Melanie Hall.
p. cm.
ISBN 978-0-7613-4495-7 (lib. bdg. : alk. paper)
1. Ten Commandments—Juvenile fiction. 2. Sinai, Mount (Egypt)—Juvenile fiction.
I. Hall, Melanie, ill. II. Title.
PZ7.R71943 li 2011
[Fic]—dc22 2010021249

PJ Library Edition ISBN 978-0-7613-8031-3

Manufactured in Hong Kong
3-44973-12302-10/25/2017

051825K3/B1202/A4

# The Littlest Mountain

BY Barb Rosenstock

ILLUSTRATED BY Melanie Hall

KAR-BEN PUBLISHING

Long, long ago God called
all of the mountains together.

"My friends," God said, "since time began, you have watched over the world with me. Some people have been kind and generous with one another, while others have been hateful and cruel. My people cannot seem to live together."

The mountains agreed. But what did God want from them?

"People have always looked up to the heavens," God continued, "so I will speak to them from a mountaintop. I will give them laws to follow so that the world will finally know peace."

The mountains cheered at this privilege. They joined in a great circle and danced.

Then God asked quietly, "Which mountain should I choose?"

Instantly, the dance ended. The mountains broke apart, pushing and shoving.

They turned this way and that, trying to impress God.

"Of course God will choose me," bragged the beautiful Mount Carmel. "My seaside slopes are lush and green. My Hebrew name means *garden.* People fight over my rich land. I'm the most important mountain."

The other mountains mumbled in protest, except for little Mount Sinai. Its slopes were far too rocky for anyone to want.

"No, God will choose me," boasted Mount Hermon. "I am broad and strong. I have three peaks. People marvel at my rushing streams and snow-capped summits. In my caves, they build temples to the sun and moon. They like me best."

The other mountains grumbled with jealousy, except for little Mount Sinai.
Its face was far too plain for anyone to like it best.

Majestic Mount Tabor pushed boldly through the crowd. "God will choose me. Remember, I kept my head above water during the great flood. I am the mountain closest to heaven."

The other mountains rumbled with memories of the flood. Still they argued, except for little Mount Sinai. Its peak was far too lowly to see the wonders of heaven.

Soon other mountains joined in the boasting.

"Valuable rocks are mined from my land," Mount Ebal crowed.

"My hills are home to the fiercest battles," Mount Moriah blustered.

"My meadows are filled with heavenly flowers," Mount Gilboa gloated.

Each mountain stepped forward to praise itself, sure it deserved the privilege of being chosen. Only Mount Sinai stood back.

"And what about you, little Sinai?" asked God. "Have you nothing to say?"

"No, God," said Sinai. "Unlike the others, I'm not a great mountain in any way. Whichever mountain You choose will be the best."

God thought.

"I do not want to speak from a mountain that is boastful and vain," said God to the beautiful Mount Carmel.

"I do not want to speak from a mountain that has been used to worship suns and moons," said God to the vast Mount Hermon.

"And I do not want to speak from the mightiest peak. My people should know that I am down among them always," said God to the majestic Mount Tabor.

Mount Sinai stepped further back to admire the massive cliffs and peaks of the other mountains. Lost in thought, it wondered which would be chosen.

"Come forward, Sinai," God called, while the other mountains squabbled among themselves.

"Yes, God?" said the littlest mountain.

"I choose you, the humblest mountain, to be the special place where I will speak to My people. For you were silent when the others were boasting. You were peaceful when the others were fighting. And only you put your trust in Me."

And so the other mountains returned to their homes, a little less full of themselves, but a good deal wiser about the ways of God.

And soon enough, God spoke to the people as promised. The Ten Commandments were given to all from the top of humble Mount Sinai, which on that day, was very close to heaven indeed.

## AUTHOR'S NOTE

This story is adapted from *The Contest of the Mountains,* a legend in the Midrash *(Bereshit Rabbah 99:1).* The ancient rabbis were trying explain why Mount Sinai was chosen as the site of the giving of the Ten Commandments. Their explanation attributes human characteristics to the mountains of the world. The locations of the mountains, however, do not all correspond to the geography of the Middle East.

Thanks to Rabbi Scott Looper for his library, his knowledge of Hebrew, and his guidance through the Midrash.

## SOURCES

Bialik, Hayim Nahman and Ravnitzky, Yehoshua Hana (eds), *The Book of Legends Sefer Ha-aggadah,* Schocken Books, Inc. 1992

*Exodus 19:20*

Frankel, Ellen, *The Classic Tales, 4,000 Years of Jewish Lore,* Jason Aronson, Inc., 1989.

Ginzberg, Louis, *The Legends of the Jews,* The Jewish Publication Society of America, 1911.

*Midrash Bereshit Rabbah 99:1*